For my wonderful sister, Nancy — C. R.

First published in the United States, Great Britain, Canada, Australia, and New Zealand in 2013
by North-South Books, Inc., an imprint of NordSüd Verlag AG, CH-8005 Zürich, Switzerland.

Distributed in the United States by North-South Books Inc., New York 10016.
Library of Congress Cataloging-in-Publication Data is available.
ISBN: 978-0-7358-4128-4 (trade edition)
1 3 5 7 9 • 10 8 6 4 2
ISBN: 978-0-7358-4153-6 (paperback edition)
1 3 5 7 9 • 10 8 6 4 2
Printed in Germany by Grafisches Centrum Cuno GmbH & Co. KG, 39240 Calbe, April 2013.
www.northsouth.com

FSC
www.fsc.org
MIX
Paper from
responsible sources
FSC® C043106

Carol Roth · Sean Julian

Five Little Ducklings
Go to Bed

North
South

"Come here, my angels," Mama duck said.
"It's time for you to go to bed."

"Clean up your toys and lower the light,
For soon we have to say good night."

The first little duckling said, "Okay.
It's been a very busy day."

The second little duckling said, "Let's go!
Let's find our jammies . . . don't be slow."

The third little duckling said, "Let's race!
Who's the quickest to wash their face?"

The fourth little duckling said, "What fun!
Get your blankets, everyone!"

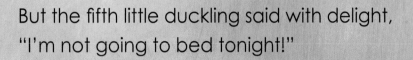

But the fifth little duckling said with delight,
"I'm not going to bed tonight!"

Then the fourth little duckling said, "Oh my,
If you're not going . . . neither am I!"

The third little duckling said, "YAHOO!
We'll stay up all night . . . that's what we'll do!"

The second and the first danced around
on the floor.
   "We're ALL not going to bed anymore!

o bedtime for us! No sleep tonight!"
nd they all went wild with a pillow fight!

The ducklings were noisy as they could be.
Mama duck said, "What's this I see?"

"Naughty little ducklings . . . what did you do?
Naughty little ducklings . . . shame on you!
Now clean up this mess!" Mama duck said.
"You have five minutes to waddle into bed!"

Five little ducklings felt so bad.
Five little ducklings felt so sad.

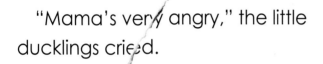

"Mama's very angry," the little ducklings cried.

And they wept on their beds as they crawled inside.

"Now, now," said Mama. "I still love you.
I always will, whatever you do.

"Sometimes you don't listen, and I get mad.
But you're my special ducklings, and I'm so glad."

"There's nothing you could ever do.
That would make me stop loving you."

"We're sorry, Mama," the little ducklings said
As she kissed them all on top of their head.

Five little ducklings hugged their mother.
Five little ducklings hugged each other.
Five little ducklings snuggled up tight
And settled down for a good, good night.